Dear Parents and Caregivers,

If your child is ready to learn how to read, then you've come to the right place! We want kids to reach for the stars as they begin their reading adventure. With Ready-to-Go!, this very first level has been carefully mapped out to launch their reading voyage.

All books in this level share the following:

★ **Just the right length: each story has about 100 words, many of them repeated.**

★ **Sight words: frequently used words that children will come to recognize by sight, such as "the" and "can."**

★ **Word families: rhyming words used throughout the story for ease of recognition.**

★ **A guide at the beginning that prompts children to sound out the words before they start reading.**

★ **Questions at the end for children to re-engage with the story.**

★ **Fun stories starring children's favorite characters so learning to read is a blast.**

These books will provide children with confidence in their reading abilities as they go from mastering the letters of the alphabet to understanding how those letters create words, sentences, and stories.

Blast off on this starry adventure . . . a universe of reading awaits!

Cat Sees Snow

written by **LAURA GEHL** *illustrated by* **FRED BLUNT**

Ready-to-Read

Simon Spotlight
New York London Toronto Sydney New Delhi

Here is a list of all the words you will find in this book. Sound them out before you begin reading the story.

Names:

Cat

Dog

Pig

SIMON SPOTLIGHT
An imprint of Simon & Schuster Children's Publishing Division
1230 Avenue of the Americas, New York, New York 10020
This Simon Spotlight edition August 2023

For information about special discounts for bulk purchases, please contact Simon & Schuster Special Sales at 1-866-506-1949 or business@simonandschuster.com.
Manufactured in the United States of America 0723 LAK
2 4 6 8 10 9 7 5 3 1
CIP data for this book is available from the Library of Congress.
ISBN 978-1-6659-2040-7 (hc)
ISBN 978-1-6659-2039-1 (pbk)
ISBN 978-1-6659-2041-4 (ebook)

Word families:

"-ow" →	blow	mow	row
	slow	snow	throw

Sight words:

can	go	in	is
no	not	so	the

Bonus words:

cannot	much	sees

Ready to go? Happy reading!

Don't miss the questions about the story on the last page of this book.

Cat sees snow.

Cat sees SO much snow!

Cat cannot
mow the snow.

Cat cannot
blow the snow.

Cat cannot
row in the snow.

Cat cannot go!

Cat is slow.

Cat is SO slow.

Dog sees snow.

Dog sees SO much snow.

Dog cannot
mow the snow.

Dog cannot
blow the snow.

Dog cannot
row in the snow.

Dog can go!

Dog is NOT slow.

Dog can throw snow.

Cat can throw snow.

Pig is slow.

Dog can throw snow.

Cat can throw snow.

NO!!!!

Pig is not slow!
Pig can go!

Now that you have read the story, can you answer these questions?

1. Which character sees snow at the beginning of the story?

2. Why is Cat slow? Why is Dog not slow?

3. In this story, you read the words "snow," "throw," "blow," "mow," "row," and "slow." Those words rhyme. Can you think of other words that rhyme with these words?

Great job!

You are a reading star!